360

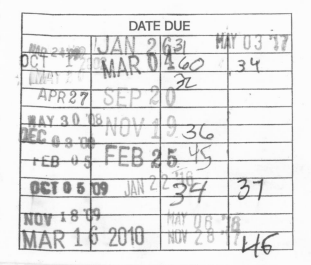

DATE DUE			
MAR 24	JAN 2 63	MAY 03 '17	
OCT 1	MAR 04 60	34	
MAY 2 0		32	
APR 27	SEP 20		
MAY 30 '08	NOV 1 9 36		
DEC 0 3 '08			
FEB 05	FEB 25 45		
OCT 0 5 09	JAN 2 '10 34	37	
NOV 1 8 09	MAY 06 '18		
MAR 1 6 2010	NOV 2 8	46	

YOUNG CAM JANSEN
and the
Lost Tooth

A Viking Easy-to-Read

by David A. Adler
illustrated by Susanna Natti

VIKING

For Charles, Jared, Jeremy, Max,
Yoni, Zev, and, of course, Eitan
—D. A.

To Colleen and Brenna Quinn
—S. N.

VIKING
Published by the Penguin Group
Penguin Books USA Inc., 375 Hudson Street, New York, New York 10014, U.S.A.
Penguin Books Ltd, 27 Wrights Lane, London W8 5TZ, England
Penguin Books Australia Ltd, Ringwood, Victoria, Australia
Penguin Books Canada Ltd, 10 Alcorn Avenue, Toronto, Ontario, Canada M4V 3B2
Penguin Books (N.Z.) Ltd, 182-190 Wairau Road, Auckland 10, New Zealand

Penguin Books Ltd, Registered Offices: Harmondsworth, Middlesex, England

First published in 1997 by Viking, a division of Penguin Books USA Inc.

3   5   7   9   10   8   6   4   2

Text copyright © David A. Adler, 1997
Illustrations copyright © Susanna Natti, 1997
All rights reserved

LIBRARY OF CONGRESS CATALOGING-IN-PUBLICATION DATA

Adler, David A.
Young Cam Jansen and the lost tooth / by David A. Adler ;
illustrated by Susanna Natti.   p.   cm. — (A Viking easy-to-read)
Summary: Cam uses her photographic memory to help
a classmate find the tooth she lost at school.
ISBN 0-670-87354-3
[1. Teeth—Fiction. 2. Schools—Fiction. 3. Mystery and detective stories.]
I. Natti, Susanna, ill. II. Title. III. Series.
PZ7.A2615Yp 1997 [Fic]—dc21 96-47357 CIP AC

Printed in Singapore
Set in Bookman

CONTENTS

1. CAM JANSEN IS NOT SILLY

"Gobble, gobble,"

Cam Jansen said.

She held up her turkey stick-puppet.

"Gobble, gobble," she said again.

Eric Shelton smiled.

"When my puppet is finished,

our turkeys can play together," he said.

4

Cam and her friend Eric

were sitting at Table Four in art class.

Annie and Robert were at the table, too.

It was almost Thanksgiving.

On the table were papers, crayons, glue,

scissors, string, beads, and feathers.

There were also bowls

of apples and popcorn.

Robert said,

"Playing with paper turkeys is silly."

"It is not silly," Cam said. "It's fun."

Eric told Robert,

"Cam Jansen is not silly!

She is very smart.

She has an amazing memory.

Cam remembers everything she sees."

Robert said, "I don't think so.

No one remembers everything."

Cam looked at the necklace

Annie was making.

Cam closed her eyes and said, "Click."

"Why did you say that?" Robert asked.

"My memory is like a camera,"

Cam told him.

"I have a picture in my head

of everything I have seen.

"'Click' is the sound my camera makes."

"I don't think so," Robert said again.

Cam smiled.

Her eyes were still closed.

"The beads on Annie's necklace

are yellow, blue, red, red . . ."

"You're peeking," Robert said.

Cam turned around and went on,

". . . green, blue, white, black,

red, red, blue, and green."

"You're right!" Robert said.

"You do have an amazing memory."

Cam's real name is Jennifer.

But because of her great memory,

people started to call her "the Camera."

Then "the Camera" became just "Cam."

"My necklace is done," Annie said.

She put it on.

Then Annie took an apple from the bowl.

She bit into it.

"Oh!" Annie screamed.

"Oh! My tooth!"

2. MY TOOTH IS GONE

Annie ran to the sink.

Eric ran with her.

He gave Annie a cup of water.

Annie washed out her mouth.

Then Eric gave her a paper towel.

Annie held the towel to her mouth

and returned to the table.

11

"You're lucky," Robert told her.

"I lost a tooth once. I put it under my pillow.

When I woke up, I found money there."

Annie took the towel from her mouth.

"That happens in my house, too," she said.

Annie looked in the paper towel.

She ran to the sink

and looked there, too.

Then she came back to the table.

"My tooth is gone," she said.

Mr. Fay, the art teacher,

took the large bell off his desk.

He rang the bell.

<u>Ding!</u> <u>Ding!</u> <u>Ding!</u>

"It's cleanup time," he called out.

Cam put the crayons in the box.

Eric put the feathers away.

Robert picked up the scraps of paper.

He put them in the recycling bag.

Annie was under the table.

She was looking for her tooth.

Mr. Fay came to Table Four.

"You did good work," he said.

"Thank you," Cam, Eric, and Robert said.

Annie looked out from under the table.

She said, "Thank you," too.

Mr. Fay picked up Cam's and Eric's

turkey stick-puppets.

"These look almost real."

He shook Cam's puppet and said, "Gobble."

He shook Eric's puppet and said,

"Gobble, gobble."

Then he put the puppets down

and went to another table.

Cam and Eric picked up the beads.

"Hey," Eric said.

"These white beads look like teeth.

Annie's tooth must be in this box."

Annie crawled out from under the table.

Eric and Annie

looked through the box of beads.

But they didn't find Annie's tooth.

3. CLICK!

Cam, Eric, and Annie

gave their smocks to Robert.

He took them to the closet

and hung them up.

Mr. Fay rang the bell again.

<u>Ding!</u> <u>Ding!</u> <u>Ding!</u>

"It is time to go back to class,"

he said. "Have a happy Thanksgiving."

Children from the other tables

walked out of the art room.

But Annie said, "I can't go back!

I still don't have my tooth."

"Don't worry," Eric told her.

"Cam and I will help you.

We will find your tooth.

We are good at finding things.

We are good at solving mysteries."

Cam closed her eyes.

She said, "Click!"

She said, "Click!" again.

Then she opened her eyes.

"I know where to find your tooth.

Come with me," Cam said.

Cam went to the closet.

Annie, Eric, and Robert followed her.

<u>Ding!</u> <u>Ding!</u> <u>Ding!</u>

Mr. Fay rang the bell again.

"You should be on your way to class,"

he said.

"Oh, Mr. Fay," Annie said.

"I lost my tooth."

Cam said, "And I know where to find it."

Cam closed her eyes.

"Click!

I am looking at a picture

I have in my head.

It is a picture of Annie

when she lost her tooth.

She was wearing an art smock

with a big front pocket.

I think Annie's tooth

fell into the pocket."

Annie found her smock.

She reached into the pocket.

She took out two beads and a feather.

"What else is in there?" Cam asked.

"Nothing," Annie answered.

There were tears in her eyes.

"I still don't have my tooth."

4. WAKE UP, CAM!

Cam, Eric, Annie, and Robert

left the art room.

Robert said, "I didn't think

you could say, 'Click,'

and find a tooth."

The children went into their classroom.

It was quiet reading time.

Cam opened her book.

But she did not read.

She was thinking about Annie's tooth.

Cam closed her eyes and said, "Click!"

"Please, read quietly,"

the teacher said.

Cam whispered, "Click."

She whispered, "Click," again.

She sat for a long time

with her eyes closed.

She thought about Annie's tooth.

Rrrr! Rrrr!

The school bell rang.

It was time to go home.

"Wake up, Cam! Wake up!" Eric said.

"It's time to go home."

Cam opened her eyes.

"I was not sleeping.

I was thinking about Annie's tooth.

But I don't know where it is."

Eric said, "We have to get our coats

and lunch boxes.

We have to get on the bus."

Cam looked at Eric.

"Lunch boxes!" Cam said.

She closed her eyes.

"Click!"

Cam quickly opened her eyes.

"That's it!

I know where to find Annie's tooth.

Annie! Annie!" Cam called.

"We have to go to the art room."

5. HERE'S YOUR TOOTH

Eric took his coat and Cam's coat

from the closet.

He took their lunch boxes, too.

Cam and Annie were in the hall.

"Wait for me!" Eric called.

"Come on, Annie," Robert said.

"Let's go to the bus."

27

"Not now," Annie told him.

"We are going to get my tooth."

Robert shook his head and said,

"I don't think so."

Then he went outside to the bus.

Cam, Eric, and Annie

went to the art room.

Mr. Fay was carrying garbage cans.

"Wait!" Cam called out.

"Do not throw away Annie's tooth!"

Cam found the garbage can from Table Four.

She reached in and took out an apple.

Only one bite was missing.

"This was your apple," Cam said.

"And here is your tooth."

Cam gave Annie the apple.

"Thank you. Thank you!"

Annie said to Cam.

Annie took the tooth out of the apple.

She put it in a paper towel.

Annie put the towel in her pocket.

Cam told Annie,

"You should thank Eric, too.

He helped me find your tooth.

When Eric said 'lunch boxes,'

I thought about eating.

When I thought about eating,

I thought about the apple.

That's when I knew

where to find your tooth."

Annie thanked Eric.

Eric gave Cam her coat and lunch box.

"If we don't hurry, we will miss our bus."

Cam, Eric, and Annie ran outside.

The bus was still there.

"I wanted to leave," the driver said.

"But Robert asked me to wait."

Cam, Eric, and Annie

thanked Robert and the driver.

Annie told Robert,

"Cam clicked and found my tooth."

Robert smiled.

"I knew she would find it," he said.

"I just knew it!"